GalenaElementarySchool
114 South Main Street
Galena, MD 21635

To puppies everywhere and the kids who love them!

About This Book

The photographs in this book were taken with a digital SLR camera, with a fish-eye lens and flash, inside a special underwater casing designed for scuba divers. However, Seth did not use scuba diving breathing equipment, since he and the puppies were only underwater for a few seconds.

This book was edited by Leslie Shumate and designed by Phil Caminiti under the art direction of Saho Fujii. The production was supervised by Erika Schwartz, and the production editor was Wendy Dopkin. The text and display type were set in VAG rounded.

Photo Credits

Jacket flaps (flag banner): RKaulitzki/istockphoto.com • Jacket front cover and spine (beach ball): popovaphoto/istockphoto.com • Jacket front flap, 8–9 (pool tile): zinchik/istockphoto.com • Jacket back cover, 6–7, 36–37 (pool tile): Mauro_Scarone/istockphoto.com • Jacket back flap, 10–11, 26–27 (pool tile): Mercedes Rancaño Otero • 4–5, 24, 30–31 (pool tile): BreatheFitness/istockphoto.com • 4–5 (beach ball): BreatheFitness/istockphoto.com • 12–13, 35 (pool water): ermingut/istockphoto.com • 16–17 (pool tile): oleksagrzegorz/istockphoto.com • 18–19 (pool tile): Matthew71/istockphoto.com • 20–21 (pool water): webphotographeer/istockphoto.com • 22–23 (bubbles): Marat Sirotyukov/istockphoto.com • 28–29 (pool water): webphotographeer/istockphoto.com • 32–33 (pool water): LisaValder/istockphoto.com

❧ Little, Brown and Company ❧ Hachette Book Group ❧ 1290 Avenue of the Americas, New York, NY 10104 ❧ Visit us at lb-kids.com ❧ Little, Brown and Company is a division of Hachette Book Group, Inc. The Little, Brown name and logo are trademarks of Hachette Book Group, Inc. ❧ The publisher is not responsible for websites (or their content) that are not owned by the publisher. ❧ First Edition: June 2016 ❧ Library of Congress Cataloging-in-Publication Data ❧ Casteel, Seth. Puppy pool party! : an underwater dogs adventure / Seth Casteel. — First edition. ❧ pages cm ❧ Summary: Photographs and simple, rhyming text reveal what goes on beneath the surface at a puppy pool party. ❧ ISBN 978-0-316-37633-4 (hc) ❧ [1. Stories in rhyme. 2. Dogs—Fiction. 3. Animals—Infancy—Fiction. 4. Swimming—Fiction.] I. Title. ❧ PZ8.3.C2796Uq 2016 ❧ [E]—dc23 ❧ 2014047874 ❧ 10 9 8 7 6 5 4 3 2 1 ❧ APS ❧ PRINTED IN CHINA

Seth Casteel

PUPPY POOL PARTY!

An **UNDERWATER DOGS** Adventure

LITTLE, BROWN AND COMPANY

New York   Boston

YOU'RE INVITED

to a puppy pool party!

The sun is out. It's time to play.

Come swim and
splash the day away!

Test
the
water.

Dip
your
toes.

Blow some bubbles
through your nose!

Slip and slide.

Float and glide.

You're in for a fun wet ride!

Run and jump.
Give it your all.

You **splash** the most when you...

Nice move, puppy! You've got style.

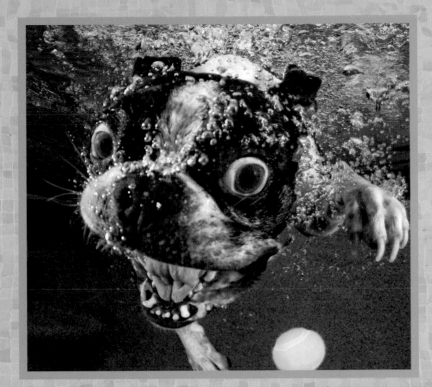

Now let's see your underwater smile.

Some pups paddle in a pair.

Swimming buddies love to share!

Safety first! It's crystal clear.

**Don't swim without
a lifeguard near.**

Doggy-paddle,
strong and fast.

Swirling
bubbles
are a
BLAST!

Try the deep end when you're ready.

You can make it—slow and steady!

Crank the music.
Howl along.

Dance around to your favorite song.

Swimming puppies
are so brave.

Surf's up, puppy!
Catch that wave.

If you're tired, take a break.

Dry off with a great big shake.

Warm and sleepy,

dream away.

What a fun
pool party day!

THE GUEST LIST

Orbit, 10 weeks

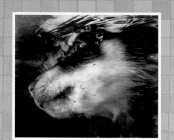

Hunter, 6 weeks

Cookie, 16 weeks

Avi, 5 months

Iggy, 15 weeks

Clyde, 16 weeks

Doc Brown, 9 weeks

McFly, 8 weeks

JR, 5 years

Buster, 6 years

Prince, 8 weeks

Jack, 12 weeks

Rocco, 5 years

Monty, 6 months

Flynn & Jenner, 3 years

Pringles & Pickme, 8 weeks

Grits & Reason, 12 weeks

Teenybopper, 7 weeks

Corey, 8 weeks

Caru, 6 weeks

Dora, 16 weeks

Atticus, 6 weeks

Simia, 9 weeks

Ruger, 7 weeks

Zelda, 8 weeks

Daisy, 5 years

Archie, 10 weeks

Pepper, 16 weeks

Ritzie, 9 weeks

Party Animal, 8 weeks

The Three Amigos, 8 weeks

Luna, 18 weeks

A NOTE FROM THE AUTHOR

To create these images, I taught swimming lessons to over 1,500 puppies, helping them to build confidence and safety skills in the water. Many of the youngest puppies only swam for a few minutes, but in that time they learned about buoyancy, their physicality in the water, and most importantly, how to get out of a pool. Some of the more adventurous puppies were instantly comfortable in the water and immediately began jumping in the pool and chasing toys! I'd like to give a big thank-you to all the amazing animal rescue organizations that helped to make this book possible by providing such wonderful puppies! Adoption is a great option!